IngramSpark is an award-winning independent publishing platform, offering the same fully-integrated print and digital products and global distribution services enjoyed by big-time publishers—superb quality and industry connections backed by decades of experience—all made accessible to the indie-publishing community through a single platform. Once you finish and format your book, IngramSpark makes it possible to share it with the world. Focus on what you do best — create innovative content — while IngramSpark does the rest: print, ship, and distribute.

The options are endless with IngramSpark's numerous formats, including dozens of trim sizes, premium color or crisp black and white, e-books, hardbacks, paperbacks, and more.

Our print-on-demand capabilities enable you to print what you need and nothing more, so say goodbye to a garage full of inventory, and say hello to readers worldwide. Not only do we print and ship your books, but we also get them where readers expect to find them. Our global distribution network connects your book to more than 39,000 retailers and libraries around the world and reaches 70+ major online channels including Amazon, Barnes & Noble, Apple, Kobo, and more.

Additionally, IngramSpark offers excellent customer service and invests in helping you become a successful self-publisher with resources such as calculators, videos, guides, blog articles, while providing you access to experts within the publishing community.

It's your content. We just help you do more with it.

If you would like to read the entire book,
you may purchase from your local bookstore or online retailer:

Queen of Chaos: Stolen Futures: Unity, Book One (Stolen Futures #1)

ISBN 9781939038623

5.5 x 8.5 in or 216 x 140 mm Blue Cloth
with Jacket and Matte Lamination

Black & White on 50# Crème Paper

Actual Book Contains 322 Pages

www.cjlyons.net

Thanks to CJ LYONS, LLC for allowing us to use this book as a sample book.

Other titles available from **CJ LYONS, LLC**

9781939038630   9781939038647   9781939038593   9781939038111

9781939038371

9781939038395

9781939038258

Perfect Bound
9781939038449
Case Bound
9781939038432

Perfect Bound
9781939038531
Case Bound
9781939038548

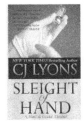

Perfect Bound
9781939038197
Case Bound
9781939038272

Perfect Bound
9781939038494
Case Bound
9781939038487

Perfect Bound
9781939038180
Case Bound
9781939038265

Perfect Bound
9781939038579
Case Bound
9781939038586

Perfect Bound
9781939038203
Case Bound
9781939038289

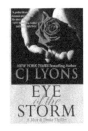

Perfect Bound
9781939038326
Case Bound
9781939038333

Perfect Bound
9781939038463
Case Bound
9781939038456

Perfect Bound
9781939038555
Case Bound
9781939038562

United States

- Via Ingram Book Group, IngramSpark titles are automatically made available to more than tens of thousands of retailers, libraries, schools, internet commerce companies, and other channel partners, including Amazon, Barnes & Noble, Chapters Indigo (Canada), and other well-known book retailers and wholesalers across North America.

United Kingdom | Europe

- Adlibris
- Agapea
- Amazon.co.uk
- Aphrohead
- Bertrams
- Blackwell
- Book Depository Ltd
- Books Express
- Coutts Information Services Ltd
- Designarta Books
- Eden Interactive Ltd
- Foyles
- Gardners
- Trust Media Distribution (formerly STL)
- Mallory International
- Paperback Shop Ltd
- Superbookdeals
- The Book Community Ltd
- Waterstones
- Wrap Distribution

Australia & New Zealand

- Booktopia
- Fishpond
- The Nile
- James Bennett
- ALS
- Peter Pal
- University Co-operative Bookshop

Our Global Print On Demand Distribution Network reaches over 39,000 bookstores, libraries and retail outlets.

STOLEN FUTURES UNITY:
VOLUME ONE,
QUEEN OF CHAOS

CAT LYONS

GET THE COMPLETE
STOLEN FUTURES:
UNITY TRILOGY

QUEEN OF CHAOS

THIEF OF TIME

PAWNS OF
DESTRUCTION

Copyright 2017, CJ Lyons, LLC

EdgyReads

Cover art: Rosario, stock images courtesy of Adobe Stock

Library of Congress Case # 1-4337024011

Published in the United States of America

"You must have chaos within you to give birth to a dancing star."

~ Friedrich Nietzsche

Prologue

EVERY NIGHT FOR the past three weeks, Annie McCoy died.

Her deaths were neither gruesome nor bloody. Rather, everything that made Annie Annie, from her cowlick that refused to be tamed to her freckles and the scar on the inside of her calf that came from shinnying up a tree when she was eight to her worries about the cute guy who sat beside her in World Cultures never noticing her—or worse, what if he did?—all those myriad microscopic moments that combined to create Annie's utterly average life, each night pulverized into dust, spiraling into a vast abyss of nothingness.

Every night. Annie's entire existence, all sixteen years, five months, four days of it, picked apart and flung to the wind, bones scoured clean by invisible carrion birds.

Leaving her exhausted body behind. Not sleeping, paralyzed. Helpless.

All night long. Trapped. Not in a dream, more like a night terror.

Loud booms and explosions, her brain a battlefield. Bits and pieces of memory unwinding, sometimes backwards, sometimes forward, sometimes random ricochets. More than remembering...re-living. Her entire life dissected like a frog.

The worst thing wasn't worrying about a brain tumor or searching for the courage to ask her parents to take her to the doctor. No, the worst thing about being forced to examine her life moment by moment each night was seeing exactly how boring her sixteen years, five months, and four days spent on the Planet Earth had been.

Unremarkable. That was Annie: dependable, reliable, trustworthy. Normal with a capital average, living life anonymously in the shadow of the bell-shaped curve.

So very unlike her brilliant father whose company flew him around the world to teach other engineering geniuses. His new quantum computer would save the world for her and generations to come, he'd tell her whenever he apologized for never being home.

Her equally talented mother held PhDs in both history and library sciences and was in charge of one of the most treasured historical archives in the western world, hidden safe miles below the surface at Iron Mountain. While Dad saved the future, Mom preserved the past.

Even her little brother was special in his own way. Nate was autistic, unable to communicate verbally, but could climb anything—*any* thing—and was a natural mimic. Birdcalls, music, voices, he was pitch perfect after hearing something once.

Annie lived her life surrounded by extraordinary people. If only she could get some sleep...then maybe she would have enough energy to actually discover something special about herself.

As it was, it took all her strength simply to drag herself through her day—especially after Dad left on his trip and Mom switched to the night shift, leaving Annie to help Nate in the morning. Get herself up, get Nate up, drive to school, sleepwalk through eight hours, then home again, Nate in tow, in time for Mom to wake up so they could have dinner together. After getting Nate settled in, Mom would head to work, and Annie would lie down, praying tonight was the night she'd finally sleep.

But no. It was as if someone was watching her. Five minutes after her head hit the pillow (in her own bed or the guest room or even Dad's comfy old recliner in the den), BAM!, the first salvo would hit. With that initial shockwave blasting through her brain would come paralysis. All she could do was lie there, disconnected from her own body and mind as her life played out behind her eyelids.

Tonight, as soon as she closed her eyes, the shriek of a

cannon ripped through her mind as her vision filled with a light so bright she winced in pain.

Memories cascaded through her awareness like white-water rapids, some as jagged and sharp as broken glass, others warm and sweet as honey on cinnamon toast, a few so faint they were mere wisps. One, dark and ominous as storm clouds, swept closer. With a thunderclap, she was dragged into it.

In the memory, she screamed her little brother's name, her throat burning with panic. She was young, only eight, and Nate was five and lost, vanished.

Her stomach churned as she swallowed her tears—Mom was already crying enough for the both of them. More frightening, Dad made no noise at all as he somehow appeared to shrink from the father who could do anything to a man made helpless and small by events beyond his control.

No. She hated this memory—at least this part of it. It was the first time Nate had run away, before anyone realized how cunning he was with locks. She tried to force her mind to fast forward, push past the scary parts.

Mom had called Dad home early from work, and they'd called the police, and everyone had gone off to search, leaving Annie home with a neighbor.

It was a brilliant spring day, the leaves just beginning to open. Annie was determined to rescue her little brother. She'd searched every nook and cranny of the back yard and the woods between their house and the neighbor's until finally she'd sat down, exhausted.

The birds were singing but their songs kept changing— not the way they usually did, and she ought to know, since Nate constantly dragged her to their feeders to watch and listen. She'd looked up through the tree branches, and there he was. She hadn't even thought twice about it, Annie scrambled up that sugar maple and brought him back down, home again safe and sound, not even noticing her scrapes and cuts the branches left in their wake.

Even to this day, she still had the scars, but they made her smile. The one time when she'd done something extraordinary, had been a hero.

The memory ended with both her and Nate wrapped in their parents' arms, happy, the way a story should end. But not tonight. Tonight, her childhood panic came back magnified a thousand fold, her chest tight, her heart ready to burst from the pressure and the never-ending terror.

She was dying. She knew it.

Blackness engulfed her, smothering her, grinding her mind and body into microscopic bits and pieces that blew into the void, scattering, shattering until she was...gone. No more. Nothing.

Her last thought, the same every single time, every single night, was: *This time, am I dead for real?*

Then, as fast as a hummingbird's wings, she was back in her own bed. Her hair stuck to her cheeks, her sheets stank of sweat and fear, her body ached from the forced paralysis. And she was tired, so very tired.

Not dead. Not this time, at least.

A pounding shook her body, bouncing it against her mattress. With one final cannon firing behind her eyelids, she blinked and was free of the paralysis that had imprisoned her body during the night.

Nate, his routine disrupted by Annie sleeping past her alarm and not coming to get him out of bed, was in complete meltdown mode, standing beside her bed, shaking her so hard her head rattled against the headboard. She grabbed him, not just to stop him, but also because when he was like this, only the close confinement of arms squeezing him tight could calm him.

He fought her, his twelve-year-old's spindly limbs lashing out, one hand slapping her. Hard enough that tears stung her eyes.

"Nate," she shouted, something she almost never did.

He jerked as if she'd been the one to slap him, but that gave her the opening she needed to grab him into a bear hug. He gasped for air, getting ready to escalate, but she squeezed tighter. It was one of the essential paradoxes that was life with Nate: the only time he would tolerate a loving touch was when he was out of control and could not register the affection. How many times had she wished to hug her little brother and just once have him return the gesture?

Annie rocked his body against hers, making small crooning noises, humming one of his favorite songs, "Blackbird" by the Beatles, and his guttural grunts of dismay slowly quieted. He stopped fighting, his breathing relaxed, and she released him.

Not for the first time, she fantasized about having the luxury of indulging in a meltdown of her own. But not today, not with Dad out of town and Mom working nights. As much as she'd love to curl up and try to sleep—really sleep—today, Nate was her responsibility.

"Time to get up," she told him.

His face eased from a tight-muscled grimace into a blank mask. These words were what started every day for Nate. Now that things were back on track, he walked to the door, waiting for her as if nothing had happened.

Annie sighed, one palm rubbing her face; she hoped it wouldn't bruise. School was impossible enough without sleep, but facing people with a black eye—again—would be a nightmare.

She closed her eyes for one blissful, tantalizing moment of quiet. To wake, just one day, without having to worry about her little brother... She opened her eyes again. Wasn't going to happen. Not until she left for college, at least. But then, who would watch over Nate? Her parents would, of course, but she couldn't help her big-sister worries...all her life she'd been Nate's protector. What would happen when she was gone?

Her entire body ached as she stepped into her slippers and shuffled with Nate down the hall and across the living room to the kitchen, where she made them both breakfast. Cocoa Puffs, no milk, and OJ for him, coffee for her. She was too exhausted to contemplate anything solid and besides, they were running late; she didn't have time. She opened her laptop to check her World Cultures presentation one last time. It was worth a third of her grade, and since she wanted to study anthropology, she was counting on Dr. Wilkerson's rec for her college applications, but she'd nailed it.

She smiled. On the laptop screen waiting for her was a

sticky note from her mother: JUST KNOW YOU'LL KNOCK 'EM DEAD! WE'LL CELEBRATE TONIGHT—TAKE OUT FROM HIGHWAY PIZZA. LOVE YA, MOM. Signed with a smiley-winky face.

Even better was the GIF waiting from Dad—somehow he'd managed to get the time zone differences right so it showed up before her presentation instead of after. He might be a genius, but telling time was not one of his strengths. She turned the laptop so Nate could see the funny kittens lip-synching "We are the Champions."

Nate ignored the kittens. Instead, he bounced in his chair, pushing his bowl away when he was done. He still wasn't back to normal after his meltdown earlier; usually he'd take his empty bowl to the dishwasher, slide it into place, third row on the top rack, then wait for her to take him to wash his face and brush his teeth. Today, he hid his face in his arms and rocked, agitated.

Maybe he wasn't sleeping either. Annie took his bowl for him and rinsed it out. A clattering noise startled her. She spun back around—Nate had spilled his orange juice directly into her laptop.

"Nate, no!" Her shout startled him, and he rocked so violently, he shook the entire table. She grabbed him, harder than she'd intended, and yanked him away from the computer. Juice dripped from every crevice, and the screen had gone blank, devouring the kittens and her project. No, no, no!

"Go sit in the living room," she ordered, sending him toward the door while she searched the counter for paper towels.

There were none. Apparently neither of her genius parents had remembered to buy any. She cursed and used the hem of her pajama top in a last-ditch effort to salvage the computer and her grade. With the help of a tea towel, she had the computer as dry as possible, even if it was sticky. She held her breath and hit the power button. Nothing. Deader than dead.

She wanted to kick the table but was smart enough not to add a broken toe to her problems, so she slapped her palm against the refrigerator instead. The sting made her feel a little better.

Dad always said that in a universe filled with infinite possibilities, everything could happen. Times like this, Annie liked to imagine an infinite number of other Annies doing exciting, wonderful things with their exciting, wonderful lives. Someday it would be her turn. Just not today.

Then she saw the clock. They were going to be so late! "C'mon, Nate," she shouted as she crossed into the living room. Nate ignored her, transfixed by his reflection in the mirror over the fireplace.

He'd taken another growth spurt recently, was now taller than her own five-two. They shared the same reddish-blonde hair and green eyes, but there the resemblance ended. Annie wasn't quite sure what she saw in her own face. Exhaustion mainly. And the red mark from Nate's slap earlier was definitely going to bruise. What fun, explaining that.

After she dropped Nate off, she could call Mom at work, ask her to let Annie stay home, a mental health day.

Not likely, but she could rebuild her presentation and maybe finally get some sleep...

Combing Nate's hair with her fingers, she placed a kiss on the air above his head—the nearest thing to affection he would allow. She never could stay angry at him for long. She sighed. "We're a pair, aren't we?"

At her voice, Nate jerked his chin up and met her gaze in the mirror. A screech of terror scratched free from him as if instead of his own sister, he'd seen a monster. He pushed Annie against the fireplace and took off in the opposite direction, arms flapping at his sides, animal noises of terror piercing the air.

"Nate, no!" Annie regained her balance and chased after him. He was headed to the front door, and if he got through it, she'd never catch him.

No lock could keep Nate in—he was fast and clever with his fingers. Before Annie could cross the living room, tripping over the coffee table and banging her shin, he had the front door unlocked and bolted outside.

Annie ran, not caring that she was still in her PJs and

slippers. Last time he'd run, he'd made it two blocks away before she'd been able to catch him—and then only because he'd stopped, transfixed by finches gathered at a bird feeder.

The neighborhood was alive with its own morning routine. The regular school bus, the one Nate had never had the chance to ride, pulled away from the curb down the block. Across the street, Mr. Carstairs backed his Volvo out of his drive. Two moms pushing jog strollers ran past, both swiveling their heads to stare at Nate as he sprinted barefoot across grass still wet with morning dew. The block was used to Nate's antics and knew better than to chase after him—it only made him more upset, sending him leaping over any obstacle, ducking past any adult in pursuit, even climbing onto rooftops or taking to the trees like one of the birds he was obsessed with.

"Nate, stop!" Words were fruitless—when Nate was like this, it was as if he was blinded by tunnel vision and had lost the ability to hear anything except his own screams.

Her slippers were slowing her down. She kicked out of them and sped up, heart pounding in her ears as Nate headed into the road. Panic lanced through Annie, so sharp it stole her breath. "Nate!"

He dropped to the pavement at the exact center of the street, hugging his knees to his chest, rocking and keening with a voice so loud and sharp it could shatter glass.

Mr. Carstairs slammed on his brakes, his Volvo screeching to a stop half-in and half-out of his driveway. "Is he okay?" he called out his open window.

"I've got him," Annie said, catching up to Nate and hugging her arms around him as she had earlier. When he went into total meltdown like this, there simply wasn't much more to be done—especially not since he'd grown stronger than she was. His shrieking stopped, but his body was still rigid, resisting any effort to move.

"C'mon, Nate," she coaxed. "We can't sit here in the street all morning. People will talk." She tried another tactic: whistling his favorite bird call, a rose-breasted grosbeck, one of his primary rewards. "Stand up, now."

He complied, whistling a tufted titmouse's song, then paused, waiting for her response.

"No more until you get back inside." She tugged on his arm, but he pulled away, dropping his weight like a stone.

Her focus totally on him, she didn't register Mr. Carstairs' warning cry. But she couldn't ignore the scream of brakes or the bright yellow wall of metal barreling down on her. In the center was the school bus's blackbird logo, wings stretched wide, stark and alone.

"Nate!" Suddenly the world around her collapsed into a kaleidoscope of light—not unlike the way her mind was wrenched and twisted by her night terrors.

But this time, she didn't see the past. Instead, for that split second where time froze, Annie saw the future. *All* the futures, spiraling out from this moment, this choice.

To fall away, save herself? Or turn the other way? Toward Nate?

Her stomach clenched with the same feeling she had while climbing and committing to a pitch beyond her ability. That moment of free fall when you swung into the air, trusting that the rock and your hands and feet were enough to defeat gravity's greedy grasp.

Now, the blackbird hurtling toward her, she saw it all: her parents weeping, neglected bird feeders, a closed casket shimmering with candlelight, a climbing harness and helmet untouched, dust and cobwebs gathering. Most of all, the silence, the overwhelming silence... The void Nate would leave in his wake.

No. That was not the future she chose.

She felt the bite of the asphalt against her naked feet as she pushed with every ounce of strength. Felt the soft worn flannel of Nate's pajama top as she strained to shove him away to safety...felt the wrenching impact of something big and fast slam into her.

All around her, blackbirds beat their wings, shrieking their dismay as they bolted into the air, a tornado of feathers sharp as metal slicing her flesh.

So high, so fast, so far... Annie flew, propelled by screams and cannon booms thundering through her brain just as they had in her nightmares.

Dying. Again. But this time felt different.

This time it felt real.

THE ADVENTURES CONTINUE IN
STOLEN FUTURES: UNITY
VOLUME TWO
THIEF OF TIME

Despite overwhelming odds, Annie has done it! She's stolen the Delphi Key from the most powerful man in Unity, Comptroller Franco Albanese.

But she lost the young dataminer who brought her to this strange new world. N-8 has been captured by Franco and taken to his Palace at Fort Knox.

Together with her newfound allies, Annie has retreated to the isolated desert oasis known as Mirage, a community built below the Mojave solar reservation and protected from Franco and his Chief Enforcer, Blake.

As she tries to decipher the mysteries hidden in the Key and decide her next move, Annie learns that there's a larger conspiracy surrounding Delphi—one that goes back over a decade and involves Revv's lost mother, her father, and Franco himself.

If Annie can't trust the people who have saved her life, who can she trust? And if she must choose between saving N-8 and the lives of the other dataminers and saving the world, how can she decide to sacrifice the boy who is so very like her own brother back home?

Will sacrificing everything she is give her the strength she needs to save the world? Or will losing her humanity condemn it?

About Cat:

Cat Lyons is the fun "little sister" pen name of award-winning, *New York Times* and *USA Today* bestselling thriller author CJ Lyons.

Both have been storytellers as long as they can remember. CJ/Cat wrote her first fantasy novel when she was fifteen followed by two science fiction novels while in med school. Her two contemporary YA thrillers (*Broken* and *Watched*) both received critical acclaim and won several awards.

Under Cat's name you'll find everything from Science Fiction to contemporary suspense...not as dark as CJ but just as edgy and filled with the "heart" that sets CJ's "Thrillers with Heart" apart from other books.

Learn more at CatLyons.net

CPSIA information can be obtained
at www.ICGtesting.com
Printed in the USA
BVHW071940230120
570352BV00002B/11/J

2 370000 535030